Prickly and Smooth

by Rod Theodorou and Carole Telford

Hammer

Contents

RIGBY
INTERACTIVE LIBRARY

© 1996 Rigby Education
Published by Rigby Interactive Library,
an imprint of Rigby Education,
division of Reed Elsevier, Inc.
500 Coventry Lane
Crystal Lake, IL 60014

Illustrations by Sheila Townsend and Trevor Dunton
Color reproduction by Track QSP
Printed in China

00 99 98 97 96
10 9 8 7 6 5 4 3 2 1

ISBN 1-57572-064-7

Library of Congress Cataloging-in-Publication Data
Theodorou, Rod.
    Prickly and smooth / by Rod Theodorou and Carole Telford;
[illustrations by Sheila Townsend, Gwen Tourett, and Trevor Dunton].
        p.   cm. -- (Animal opposites)
    Includes index.
    Summary: Compares the habitat, feeding patterns, and behavior of the
porcupine and tortoise as determined by their physical attributes.
    ISBN 1-57572-064-7 (lib. bdg.)
    1. Animals--Juvenile literature. 2. Porcupines--Juvenile literature.
3. Turtles--Juvenile literature. 4. Anatomy, Comparative--Juvenile literature.
[1. Porcupines. 2. Turtles] I. Telford, Carole, 1961-   .
II. Townsend, Sheila, ill. III. Tourett, Gwen, ill. IV. Dunton, Trevor, ill.
V. Title. VI. Series: Theodorou, Rod. Animal opposites.
QL49.T348 1996
591.5--dc20   95-41625
                                                                   CIP
                                                                    AC

Photographic Acknowledgments

Anthony Bannister/OSF p4; Christian Grzimek/Okapia/OSF p5;Vivek R Sinha/OSF p6 *t*; Daniel J Cox/OSF p6 *bl*;
Alan Root/OSF p6 *br*; David Curl/OSF p7 *t*; Tsuneo Nakamura/OSF p7 *b*; Michael Fogden/OSF p8 *l*;
Frank Schneidermeyer/OSF p8 *r*; Tui De Roy/OSF pp9, 17; Bob Bennett/OSF p10; Stephen Dalton/OSF p11;
Mike Kraetsch/OSF p12 *l*; Joe Mcdonald/OSF p12 *r*; G I Bernard/OSF pp13, 21; Robert Lubeck/OSF p14;
Steve Turner/OSF p15; Partridge Films Ltd/OSF p16; Gregory K Scott/Photo Researchers/OSF p18 *l*;
Joan Root/OSF p18; Mark Jones/OSF p19; Leonard Lee Rue/Photo Researchers/OSF p20; Mike Linley/OSF p21 *r*
Front cover: Alan Root/OSF; Konrad Wothe/Bruce Coleman Ltd

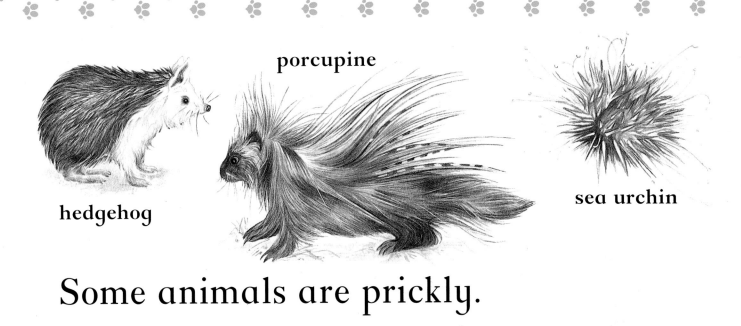

porcupine

hedgehog

sea urchin

Some animals are prickly.
Some animals are smooth.

snake

dolphin

tortoise

This is a porcupine.
Porcupines have prickles on
their backs.

This is a tortoise.
Tortoises have hard, smooth shells.

There are different kinds of porcupines. Some live on the ground and some live in the trees.

common porcupine

North American porcupine

tree porcupine

There are different kinds of tortoises. Some are small and some are huge.

bowsprit tortoise

giant tortoise

7

Some porcupines live in rain forests.
Others live in hot deserts.
Furry porcupines live in cold forests.

Tortoises always live in hot places.
If they get too cold, they will die.

Porcupine prickles are called quills.
They are very sharp.

Tortoise shells are hard.
They are heavy, so tortoises
move very slowly.

Porcupines can lift up their quills.
This stops animals from eating them.

quills hidden

quills raised

Tortoises can pull their heads and legs into their shells.
They are safe from enemies in their hard shells.

Porcupines have long, sharp teeth. They have claws to help them climb.

Tortoises have thick, scaly skin.
They have a strong beak, but no teeth.

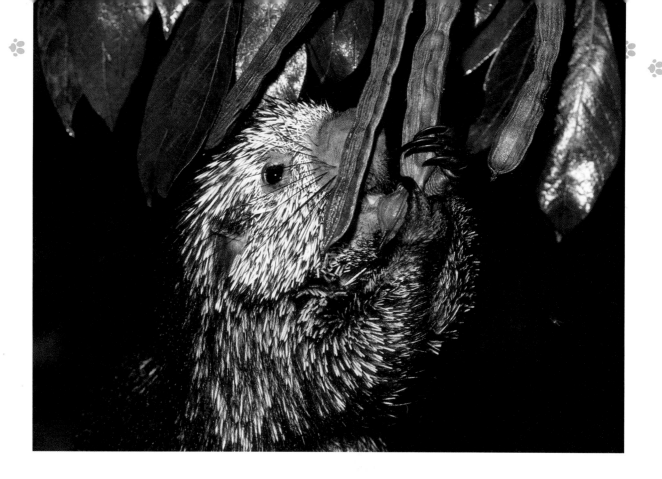

Porcupines eat leaves, berries, and fruit.
They chew the bark off trees.

Tortoises eat fruit and plants.

Some porcupines make
a den to live in.
Sometimes they live
in caves.

18

Most tortoises do not need to make a nest.
They carry their homes on their backs!

Mother porcupines have two
or three babies.
They are covered in soft fur.

two-week old baby

Mother tortoises lay lots of eggs.
A baby tortoise
hatches out
of each egg.

AMAZING FACTS!

Porcupines chew bones to sharpen their teeth.

A porcupine's teeth never stop growing!

Giant tortoises can live for more than 100 years!

One giant tortoise can weigh as much as 4 people!

Index